My name is **Mark Pett,**

and

THIS IS MY BOOK!

Alfred A. Knopf
New York

I am the author,
and that means I get to write
all of the words.

I am also the illustrator,
so I get to make all of the pictures, too.
Here, I'll draw something.

This is Percy the Perfectly Polite Panda.
He's going to help me explain the rules
of my book.

I drew you.

I get to name you.

I prefer to
be called Spike.

(*ahem*) As I was saying . . .

Rule #1: My book needs to stay nice and clean.

Look around at these spotless white pages.
Aren't they lovely? Let's keep them that way.

Rule #2: Only I get to . . .

Who colored in

my book?

Did YOU do this? You did, didn't you?

What did I say about keeping my book nice and clean?

Listen, you. You are breaking the rules.

Stop coloring in
MY BOOK!

Now, I think you'd better . . . IT'S YOU??!!

What do you think you're doing?

I'm adding some color to these boring white pages.

This is MY book. I get to decide what color the pages are.
And I say the pages are clean and white!

Oh dear, I wonder where
I left my chartreuse crayon.

Now, let's try again with fresh, new pages.

Back to **Rule #2:** As the author, only I get to write the words.

THE QUIET, NOBLE PANDA ENJOYS EATING BAMBOO.

Hey! I didn't say that!

I thought they might enjoy learning some panda facts.

I'M the author. I'm the only one who gets to write the words.

Now, **Rule #3:** As the illustrator,
I get to draw all of the pictures.

That means that no one else can . . .

HEY!

I added some
new characters!

No! You don't get to add characters!
I'm the illustrator, so I get to draw
all of the characters.

This is Pinky, Joe,
and their friends
Norbert and Squiggly,
visiting from Oregon.

Pleased to
meet you!

Arrgggh! This is so
FRUSTRATING!

Hey, guys!
I have an idea!

THIS IS MY BOOK!

But it's not just
your book.
It's ours, too.

Your book?

And it's
their book, too.

Theirs?

Well . . .

I suppose I . . .

don't have to be . . .

in charge of . . .

EVERYthing . . .

Come on.
Let's finish
the book together.

You help us,
too!